Cold Soul Demands

To Stacey
with all my love
Dave

Cold Soul Demands

By Dave Daly

Cover design and art by Michael Diflorio

Published by Green Boat Press
P.O. Box 135
Manlius NY, 13104
editor@greenboatpress.com

ISBN 0-967-1411-2-5
Library of Congress Control Number 2003116222

"A man's social and spiritual discipline must answer to his corporeal. He must lean on a friend who has a hard breast, as he would lie on a hard bed. He must drink cold water for his only beverage. So he must not hear sweetened and colored words, but pure and refreshing truths. He must daily bathe in truth cold as spring water, not warmed by the sympathy of friends."

Henry David Thoreau

Cold Soul Demands

Mirage

An empty barn is dying down,
wood hanging
on an absence of horses and hay.

A rusted plow sits inside -
and a cracked pulley
for mice to play with.

Something has breathed out
and now the wood is turning
green under the dust.

Retreating to forest.
Sinking to earth.
May it die alone for twenty years
sore and slow in our minds.

The Stoppage of Running Thoughts by a Waitress Delivered

i worried at the counter
my cup fiddling to
the radio listening while
the waitress
smiling her tilted head
to the grill returned
daughter of jesus sweet
bible reading i notice
a feeling- blessings lemonade
cigarettes notwithstanding pretty
and giving potatoes i felt time
for her
i would give my life- sorry-
not having more –return-
i would try again
her smiles did relieve
the day flirting it wasn't
a dream a blessing i believe again
i'll say it she gave me
thinking no more of dying
too much has been written

Driven by the Whiteness of the Moon

A white sea in the sky
breaks slowly around the moon,
a firm circle of light
in the swelling darkness.
You stand on the porch
listening to wind chimes,
watching the distance grow immense.
Your mind recedes before it,
taking its little furies little frights,
leaving your eyes to deal with the moon
your body frozen.
The familiar silence fills you
and you dream of that gray oak tree,
of waking and staring at red hills,
or of gulls floating in the bay.
You dream of all the other times you vanished
or became stone under the moon.
You are held by internal lights,
ancient and perfect.

Diggers Talk

Heard this:

"Two more feet. Six on the other side.

Got a light? Cold one be nice.

Here. No, the poster, y'know the tongs.

Yeah. Fuck it, other way. O.K.

Up, got it? Shit. Third time.

Told you about that bastard.

Nah, never happen. Not today anyhow.

Three hours at least.

Oh, man you gotta be kiddn. Ouch.

Just toss it, nice. Too much, too much.

Left a little, six and a quarter maybe.

Yeah. What do YOU want?"

"They told me to work with you guys."

Huh. Here. Start there. No, there.

No, THERE!

"But there's a tree in the way."

Shit, Like this, O.K.? Good.

"How far should I go?"

Six.

"Six what?"

Feet!

Now what?

"I'm measuring six feet."

CHRIST! You believe this?

Well, how would you do it?

JUST DIG.

October Presence

A breath that is not
arises from the pine shadows
and from the sun on the grass.

Down the silent slope goes the empty breeze.

How did the dandelions grow
beneath my denim crossed legs?

When I put my hand on the bark
nothing happens in this world.

But there is something watching.

It likes me to sit beneath this tree
on this hill in this afternoon,
and it likes me to watch the flies, the ants
maples black squirrels sparrows and oaks.

Thankful to the crickets, me and it are.

Crackling bark dusts my hands,
two burrs in my socks rest,
pine cones have landed everywhere.

The negative bloom of October:
tremulous, vibrant death.

Rapt

When your lips opened to laugh, I was close,

nose on your breast and heart in my throat.

The sounds in your throat were, ah

quick and fertile,

they made everything young and, ah

good.

That's why I tried to make you repeat it

by tickling, by licking.

I want so much of you.

Liberry Skollurs

Big-high rows a books, words
In the liberry, me with my glasses
Makin m'eyes water. Watching
As Rebokkin squeak squeak comes

Frined o mine Bill by name,
Wait no it's a other kid,
Frecklesweat t-shirt, lookin
For's pardner, here, by chance?

Brightly, hotly, hide and peek
Good cover those books,
He spots, sees, runs.

It's all silent oral-wise
But hear the slap-slap

Rumble and shakin metal,

Those books make a hell

Of a scar I think.

Nickel soup, dollar-a-bottle-

Man jumps in his corner,

Affrighted by the noise,

He's a mad

Reader of god knows what.

Here comes a mama barge

Towing sister float beyind.

Nawmally threatful, she's a little

Havin trouble, pickina fight

With this ol liberrio.

She's a 7-11 lady with pain from books

The little girl tries to ease.

"Books in school" girl say from the wake

But momma's cruising for the gamester boys.

Shoppers random by, finding
This marketing scheme confusing.
The stacks remain intimidational, specially
To daddies all insurance
They throw republican darts at
The woodbee thinkers.
Can't let em jus sit ere and read, eh?

Who me?
Ahm just lookin for a recipea
Cheese sueflay
And maybe a girl 'f one's around.

A Day Inside

Is there something I may make with still air
at the time when I sit in a blue room?
I cannot smoke cigarettes forever.
Nor can I tap my fingers to life's beat
when its movement is not apparent here.
The angry buzz of cars fills my window
it seems to be dancing with the gray smoke
it makes me want to throw my face in it.
A radio worries at me from next door
and the whirling, thrashing of my mind
is evident only in a small finger
moving in a circle on my dead thigh.
Bugs stuck in amber are parked everywhere
and even the wind never blows, really.

Saturday Morning

The glow is in everything,
I breathe it this morning.
My mother's plants are singing in the window light,
the antique chair is skipping
in time with the beating walls
and the musty green sofa dances
with rhythm from the gyrations of the dreaming dog.
The rocking chair sprinkles holy water
over our heads as we laugh,
the lamps harmonize, and the books
spring from the shelves in a frantic jig.
Paintings glide up to the ceiling
playing, singing butterflies, birds,
the blue carpet does its grass imitation,
the brown table rears back and roars
and smiles
the curtains sizzle in the sun,
the Saturday celebration has begun.

Dave Daly

Museum Tripping

(a visit to the Metropolitan, and a Daily News story)

Michael and Rhona Koral
called the cops
to settle one of their spats,
late Wednesday night.

A smooth plaster woman
rests her dusty hand
in a pile of wooden antiques.

I see the music of shattered cellos
when a full woman clings to ash
with her fake jewels,
knives with faces on the handles,
in the impossible multicolored chicken wire
box.

There are phalluses everywhere.
Invisible waves strain the invisible pier
while the jumble of bones, the patriot
shakes his red, white and blue.

Police dispatched a squad car
to the Korals' home,
a $3 million, 14-room colonial mansion.

I am fired by shiny metal and trip
over Columbus' head wrapped in a map
while the immobile mutant watches,
his beautiful eyes are ball bearings
sliding through marble sludge.

A severed breast makes me sweat,

the genitals are always so vague,
purple fruit is always a stimulant.

Although the Korals are divorcing
they have continued to share
the palatial digs.

I turned a corner and saw
technology, circuits, cities in mid-air
abstract enough to love beyond utility.
Minus people, stained
and draped with shadows.
They can't quite abstract the flesh.

He was booked on harassment, Rhona
was angry he wouldn't move the Lincoln
from the Jaguar's parking space.
She was booked on assault
for slapping him in the head.

A little green goblet, by its very presence
tortures a pretty vase of white flowers.
Still life become haiku
if you gaze long enough.

Pictures always whore the subject
when we think of the photographer.
I go through a garden of rocks,
hearing metal. A blank canvas, a meditation.

Buddha stands in an artichoke
perfect round head, bald, belly,
and I laugh at elephant art.
My friend Joann is by the window
sculpture foreground,
Fifth avenue background.

I've gotten these calls thirty-one times
Sgt. Post said. Michael denies it,
says it was only twenty times.

Sheets of glass spin, circles in, out.
Yellow cubes define avenues.
Furs and facepaint, barbarous jewels
glitter on the perfect
destruction of the beggar,
Portrait in gray.

Lights hang their messages out.
Disembodied faces float, abstract flesh.
There are abutments, lions, triple angles
doors and windows splashed everywhere,
honks, whistles, an encompassing hum.

I see gray light, a sliver of sun, breasts,
fat men with aprons and brooms.
A flash of music goes by in a box
gray birds watch from every corner
clocks work in the cliffs, reflections
puddles here and there,
wavering walls of people.
I take my steps, out.

Michael gets the den and the living room,
Rhona gets one bedroom exclusively.
They share the refrigerator,
but the judge ordered Rhona
to leave Michael's cantaloupes alone
and Michael to leave Rhona's grapes alone.

Point of reference, here, page,
between ears too,
a million speckles inclusive.

A Cold Night at Home

In the melting of lamplight
my dog lies still;
a pool of yellow fur,
she stretches the blue
of sorry winter evening.
I write late, swearing and scribbling
silence on a white page
under a bare bulb,
but she breathes different air
and more slowly, with sour, Eden breath.
Sometimes I hold her head and plead for help
but she won't get up, and only yawns
Then I stand back and watch her
chin in a smoothe embrace with the sofa
and I turn away covered with her dreams.

Inside a Drunkard's House

If you look through the front door
you can see the ceilings are high enough
for the ugly shadows and intricate daydreams
to moil and swoop like bats
over the neglected furniture
and return suddenly to the corners
to wait in irrelevance and wonder
if there will be any visitors soon.
The walls in these rooms are gray plaster
with deep scars under patches
of half-hearted repair
that continue to shower dust.
The windows have white curtains,
attractive replacements for the morning sun
always laughing and yelling outside,
showoff that he is,
but the windows contain him
they know about such intruders
and the damage they can do.
The carpet has been carefully chosen and laid,
it will not stain
lamps can fall without sound
without breaking, and the meditations
of the earnest and dull tables and chairs
will not be disturbed.
These rooms usually serve
as bulwarks against the demanding space
of the close inner rooms.

Further in, where neighbors have never been
the stairway is painted purple and gold
with a plastic chandelier

and wood rails with angels carved in them
ever ready for a glorious ascent.
The bedrooms hold dusty books, fading paintings
and televisions, all unplugged
reserves, in case the morning doesn't (it tragically always
does) come.

Down below in the basement
where only the drunkard himself has been,
a vault filled with knives
whetted for penance,
mounted, but loose and ready
for lashing at the walls or stairs
when they become indistinct
as they tend to do.
There is only one other room in the house, and
the hallways leading to it are long and dark.
Passing through them is hard,
takes desperation and concentration.
It is the kitchen, a jaundiced yellow,
barren except for the cabinet
seven foot high in the middle of the floor.
The precious ambrosia in the lonely shrine
rests in bottles of colored glass.
Light sneaks out from cracks in the wood,
struggling to bring joy and rest
to the cranky house,
the shabby house
set back from the road
that leads to the estranged town
and its forgotten, faded square
miles and miles away.

Estrella

The city is having its fractured sunset-
shadows crossing and falling
the large grey buildings first,
then the smaller black ones.
Light drips through the concrete maze
to smooth the eyes of Estrella
in the doorway of her little building
holding on to a broken railing
her fingers scratching the paint
from the fading, splintered wood.
She watches the cars shuttle past
and thinks of all the people inside
all these lives moving by,
she squints at the colors and shapes
and begins to mutter softly,
"indigo, rojo, amarilla".
Wondering about her grown-up children
somewhere out there in the streets
she squints and whispers
"Julio, Indio, y Maria".
She tries to imagine what part
of the sunset they can see
or if they can still remember their mother
standing in this broken-up doorway.
Go back Estrella, go back from the street
to that dark kitchen where you still
cook for four on Sunday,
where you can say the rosary
without interruption from the day.
Pray to your Lord, Estrella
but don't ask the city again
don't weep in the sunset again,
from the shadow of my balcony, tonight
I can't bear it.

Eyes

Surrounded by bones, sunk in our faces
they are crossed by a mask of red lines of blood.
Half the time they are wrapped in flesh
wreathed with delicate hair.
Eyes pull the sky to the ground
drink the moon from a pond
put love in chairs and old shirts
and blister the stranger with fire.
They draw everything in
never seeming to see God
without the power of Mind,
insatiable sister that must be fed
in the cold and the dark.

Eyes are alive
Eyes hunt
Eyes pray
Eyes make agreements
begin all love affairs and
Eyes never wait for the mind, soul, and heart,
Eyes get to it all first
and what have they done
by the time we catch up to them?

The Evening Garden

From the garden beneath my window
through the dark glass
I can feel waves of infinity,
a green universe
in the blue air of the moon,
cathedrals in the arching leaves.
The grass blows in the shadows
and a race of holy animals stirs in the night
a whisper from this dimension,
they are the poets that have died,
born again in a garden in Queens.
In the writing of starlight on the flowers
I find the eloquence of their silence.

Leaving Guilty

Let me place this crystal bowl here
put purple and white flowers in this vase
pull the curtains throw open the window
straighten the cushions on the couch
gaze at the red tropical fish
take a long slow breath
turn around once or twice
kiss your wet cheek
and then I am gone.

Discovering a Man in My Poem

A man is looking at a chair, thinking:
"This is a brown wood chair
with three rungs on the back of it,
it is chipped on one leg
another leg wobbles,
it is an old chair
brought to this country during the war
in the bottom of a big freighter
with smokestacks painted white
and seagulls on the railings,
it went through the water very fast
the Atlantic ocean with lots of fish in it
some of which are bass with brown skins and stripes
very tasty, the fishermen haul them in
and bring them to the city to sell
under a sign in a market
most of the signs are scarred and beaten
from rocks thrown by kids
fierce kids that are never in school
those old, yellow brick schools
with bells, fences, grates
monkey bars and slides
that have glass under them
coke bottles or whiskey bottles
with labels with designs on them
usually flowers and fruit,
gardens, butterflies, fairies
sunshine, birds and leaves
and all manner of little and lovely things..."
You see how this goes don't you?
You see how this could go on forever?
You see the war in line 7?

You see the ocean, the city, the fierce kids, the glass?
You see how a man in a poem,
looking at a brown wooden chair
can evade these important things
to look at only the quirks and particulars?
Who is this man and where does he come from?
Why is he in my poem, making a mockery of it?
Why should I expect him to speak of the war?
Is it me that should make him do so?
What would he do if I were in jail,
ran out of ink, or got very depressed?
Where would he go?
Would he uncover his face
if I weren't looking?
Well, I'll give him a wife and a dog
tear him from his reverie, make him speak,
I'll make him sound like an insane poet,
that's what I've got to do,
I suppose I'm responsible for him
I suppose it's my chair, and
he's one of my children.

The Moment Before Spring

The falls have long been frozen blue
tight waves, hills of tundra.
A fragile silence hangs
from the heavily posed white tips,
but, there is light in the drops
that slip from the roots hanging
over the banks.

A jay hawk clings to a thin branch, nearby,
dipping, rising, swaying in the wind
carefully watching the brush below.
The cardinals returned this morning
they lit in the branches and called
up the valley, before the hawk.

A pair of deer prints edges the snow
By the stream's unwavering gurgle
the wind brushes the rocks, then leaves
sun holds the gray trees, waits in the air.

Titled Clever Suits

Slippy and catchy here
where the opening eyes
have it, though else
will do, nicely.

Rhythm establishment di-dum
di-dum et cetera, now the real
stuff the nation wide
segment of news begins. Ballet.

If I were good this would
be apish, dwarfish, clownish
or maybe some first hand
madness, sells. Twists.

Now some little tricksy
acksydemics, draw lace
cartwheels down the page
rippity, rippity.

Fifth splatter is where
the listening tires, spinning
slower, I think we're ready
for the end, nothing said, but, sale.

Music for the Fall

Do you hear the songs in the wind?
They are gray sonnets written in smoke
proudly drawing the red and yellow leaves
from their earthly lives
in the tangled branches of the crusty oaks.
These weathered flowers sail in a new realm
you can almost hear the wild oboes
reaching airily, tumbling happily down.
Do you hear a French horn,
or the rarest of dusty, red violins
easing the trees to their rest
resplendent with melodic dreams
of the flight of the wild geese?
Autumn's a solemn symphony
erasing summer's frivolous love song.

William's Voices

From a cheap folding chair, I watch
the tense ring of faces of
the abyss-loving somnambulists.
They echo each other's chattering dreams,
wring their hands and return to the watchful trance.
The gulf between us is trembling with orphan's desire.
I am trying to kill them all with a fever
I keep in my shaggy skin,
as we smoke on and on under the bulb's light.
A freeze-dried sister speaks and we stay in our chairs:

"It was like YKNOW I could never YKNOW
express my feelings YKNOW because YKNOW
I always had this YKNOW image of myself
YKNOW that was really YKNOW terrible
and I thought that people were YKNOW looking
at me like YKNOW I was a murderer YKNOW
and I had no YKNOW sense of security
YKNOW and when my son was killed
YKNOW I couldn't sleep for two weeks YKNOW
and I began YKNOW having hallucinations
YKNOW but now YKNOW I just YKNOW pray
and YKNOW all those feelings go away
and YKNOW I have these dreams now YKNOW
where my son is YKNOW alive and in a way
YKNOW he really is YKNOW and I'm so
thankful YKNOW that I have a chance
YKNOW to live again, YKNOW it's like
for the first time I've done something
for myself YKNOW and God has YKNOW
taken care of me YKNOW
and I'm looking at the world around me YKNOW

like YKNOW a new baby YKNOW
and it's just ... well ... YKNOW incredible YKNOW ...
YKNOW."

I roll the word around on my tongue, half asleep, happy
to have found it, grateful
to seize it from her.
Without warning I am gripped by a word
from my long hatred, from my life as a six year old.
"ALYERTENUHMING"

It sailed into the void, ringing.
It came through me.
"ALYERTENUHMING"
I twitched under the prisoner's sheets, the cot
in my father's room,
I wept and plotted his death, choking
a guttural "AL, AL, AL" until
it filled me with sleep.
I dreamt of the Vandal king that night
screaming "AL, ALEEE, ALAAAAGGHH!" as he
mashed the Roman skull with a bone.
"ALYERTENUHMING"
It tolled in the solar waves.
It came into me.
I pressed hard on my bruises and foamed deep
in my belly as the shame
of dawn and speech approached,
with the little school where I learned
of "other" and slipped into silence.
"ALYERT, ALYERT, ALYERT, ALYERT"
until I could die in sleep,
fatherless.
I dreamt of a druid standing, that night,
over the dewy field where the dead lay
and whispering "ALYERTEN", and "ALYERTEN"
with trembling hands clasped.

"ALYERTENUHMING"
It carried me through the abyss, it had always
been with me.
The oak trees were dark, slow, evil
that night by the window
and my very sweat was alive with fear.
Defenseless little nerve that I was,
I repeated my word over and over
until I smothered in sleep.
In those dreams they called me "ALYERTENUHMING"
from their knees among the golden flowers.
They wore watery robes of blue, we built
bridges of silver and pine, the sky
was gold.
I laughed and loved,
the blue haired king,
son of the gods,
bringer of dawn.

"ALYERTENUHMING!"
It is the first word I have spoken since 1963
and the group looks up,
love of the abyss waking in every heart
marvel in the glory of my word, the power of my voice.
I toss them a piece of forever,
and return to my ward singing
into the void, healed,
restrained and nailed.

The Heron

At the end of the evening the rabble
shuttled off to the east
in a single monotonous blur
"only a test, only a test"
and then nothing.

Fancy shoes in the sand, 'evening dress'
striding, west, past the rubbish green
trim of beach houses in the moonlight. I am not alone.
My wife is somewhere right beside me.

A young blue heron
silhouette in the shining water.
In bow-tie I watch, stricken
"It must be breathing, it must."

A slender leg stretched forth
and the shadow head bobbed.
Rippling purple in the water, in the sky.
"This crane is dripping alive."

Satan

Satan is a reasonable man.

A red man, a hoof, a tail, a fork.
Scary? Not so. We here don't fear
big, red brutes. We love em. Sexy.

Ah, but the goatee, the pince-nez?
An eloquent tone and polished nails
keep me in my bed at night.

Satan is a reasonable man.

In Salem those women were natural
screaming and dancing mothers
till the court of law
put the divil in em.

Satan is a reasonable man.

I been in asylums and prisons
and I tell you they're very organized things.
Not by the inhabitants mind you. Madness?

Satan is a reasonable man.

My cousin's father sold insurance.
Insisted his son wear blue blazers.
Today, he is the king of Gomorrah.

Satan is a reasonable man.

He's got all the angles, all bets hedged, ducks in a row, cleanly
pressed suits and forms all filled out in triplicate.
Don't mess with him.

Meditation by Sheepshead Bay

I bring my problems to the sea
where the shifting lights in the water,
blue footprints of saints and lords
are elusive and daring statements of the moment.
The cotton tips of waves, smooth
over the brown stones on the shore
leave a sweet scent in my head.
They speak to the unruly choir inside
telling them how to hold a pose,
where to rest their eyes, and
placing them in a restive, ornate cathedral.
The wind will instruct them in rhythm
so they can sing without the usual discord,
hymns of praise that will echo in my heart
years and years after I have left the sea.

Urban Reverie at Dawn

Light comes up under dirty feathers of pigeons
sustaining a cool breeze
ruffling newspapers in the black streets.
An occasional taxi whispers past
neon lights die, two by two
heat gathers in sidewalk vents
bottles kick around
and a gray light rolls down alleys filled with dust.
This is the hour of sleep before dawn
its face swollen and sullen.
I am out and walking
as people rise carefully
to reach for the coming day,
to whisper over wooden floors,
to stare through dark windows at a trembling sun
to breathe the dawn spiraling over the buildings,
and to stretch gently in the purple light.
But today blue birds will fly through the streets,
waves of green leaves will flutter over the bridges
a flood of ancient music
will wash over the city
brown owls will wing to the towers to roost
singing will be heard from the windows
and finally I will sink in
to a deep, breathing sleep.

Dave Daly

Youths

A gang of eight year olds
leaped on my car at a stop light
laughing and pointing
at the insect frozen inside.

Afraid to run them over
I watched them swarm
over and around each other
hammering
on the hood.

A face floated into focus
on the glass, in front of me.
cherub, I'd seen him in Renaissance paintings;
red cheeks, curly hair, shining eyes,
never hurt, never cries.

His lips were curled,
after-school smile,
a little wild man
in the suburban streets.

Then he sneered like a jackal
as he ripped out my aerial.
The pack bounded away howling,
through a quiet yard
filled with leaves and twigs,
over a rotting fence.

I didn't chase him.
I knew he was headed home
to dinner where his mother would say
"How was your day, honey?"
and he'd mumble "Fine" to his peas.

Grid Hang Poem Mantra

Child	open	eye	period.
	Time		
Eye	swallow	world	Period.
	Space		
I	birth	Life	period
	?		
Life	swallow	me	period
	Sentence		
Agent	Action	Object	period
	Bloom		
God	swallow	period	God
	Meditation		
God	period	God	swallow
	Mandala		
Period	God	swallow	God
	Action		
Swallow	God	God	period
	Action		
God	God	God	period
	Action		
God	god	god	god
	G O D		

Cold Soul Demands

Get yourself some attention here personals:

Don't sing to me Maria
Unless you listen stone.
I'm not the Macy's.

Don't paint my picture Edgar
Without at least blood the brush.
Aren't either a bus station.

Don't trail me down Pete,
It needs mastiffs, oh thirty.
Never here Yellowstone parking lot.

Don't me think at all
Lest I visit in the night you.

I'm not even or close

To a Christmas tree.

Make whistle, fall down Sue

And be Jailed. I'll dance

Outside your cell.

Just for you.

I'm not banana bread I tell you.

Think about your eatings,

Mind your bearings,

Plow, for once, the lotus under.

Give the thought, now,

Before you come to me.

Be out of history, hard.

On a Lonely Beach

Holding warm sand,

tapping feet slowly

staring at the boats

and whistling sadly.

The dunes in shadow,

as the sun goes down

it cries into the blue.

The wind creeps about shyly,

the gulls are silent and gentle,

the waves whisper softly,

they remember her too.

All is One, Baby

Lemme tell ya baby, how opening night of a Broadway show on Saturday night in New York City

is the same thing as sitting in a field in a fog-filled-farm valley under a wild white half-moon

no matter who the sack of skin you think you are, is,

cuz first of all you paid for that seat baby, you paid for that seat,

and it's only you sittin' there, only you, only you.

Spruce stands alone in the watery air obscuring the stream,

seriously real.

Tree line evolves from the sifting mist and dissolves again

the breath sucks wetness and a cow moans the vanishing of its home

and there's a wonder in the air about what could be sneaking up in this blankness.

A single stalk of weed appears in the field and ducks down again

a car on the far road susshes away pushing a little blob of almost-light in front of it and a breeze starts to ply the shroud away from the grass

while you drum your fingers baby, on the chair, drumming your fingers on the chair.

you think maybe you should stand up but the mist is still there and that moon

is fixated on you baby, fixated right in your eyes and bathing your face so you just can't move

the unbearable beautiful strain of it, being held and wanting to run but not moving, baby

that's what it's all about, because you know this is all going to be gone soon

and then baby you're just lookin' at a dark field of 'falfa and another of corn,

with nothin' more to think about than when they gonna harvest and damn baby gotta go ta work tomorra.

So you got on your finest velvet fluff and yer shoes are shiny and painful

it makes you the right kind of Saturday night edgy

suddenly the lights dim and rise, dim and rise, and baby you zoom your eyes in

it's about to begin, baby,

Seriously real.

A man comes on stage and speaks with beautiful tone to a painted golden tree

a half-curtain slides back to reveal a tall, blonde woman watching the man and she cries, baby,

because they have loved and touched each other and there's a lost chance, it's gone, just gone.

The music you hadn't noticed sweetly slowly tickling the back of your head changes

and deep piano bangs rise from the pit and the man and the woman tense

a dark-haired man appears in a window behind the woman and then he vanishes

and the story becomes known as one of the only five stories that ever were

while you drum your fingers baby, on the chair, drumming your fingers on the chair.

You think maybe you should cough but you hold off, because the great song is just ending

and all will be revealed, it's all bein' revealed baby.

They're talking about us up there baby, it's all about how we are

and we watch it endlessly over and over and over again everywhere every day all the time

we can't look away from the story about ourselves and that's what it's all about watching ourselves and wanting to run but holding still, baby, until we see the finish again,

we have always got to sit still for the finish.

It's all seriously real - we're making it all up - the tension and attention is all us - on us around us.

Baby.

Contact Us:

Green Boat Press
P.O. Box 135
Manlius, NY
editor@greenboatpress.com

or join our Reader's forum at

www.greenboatpress.com